Tales from Duckport

Back to School? Cool!

by Suzy Spafford

Level **2** Reader

READING LEVEL
GRADES 1 TO 3

Published by Dalmatian Press, LLC. All rights reserved.
Printed in Luogang, Guangdong, China.

The DALMATIAN PRESS name is a trademark of Dalmatian Publishing Group,
Franklin, Tennessee 37068-2068. 1-866-418-2572. DalmatianPress.com
No part of this book may be reproduced or copied in any form without written permission
from the copyright owner. CE13175/0113

It was the first day of school
in Duckport.

"Now I look like a second-grader,"
Suzy Ducken said proudly.

Suzy walked to school with her
best friend, Emily Marmot.

"Red, blue, or purple hair bow,"
said Emily. "What do *you* think?"

"I think you're driving me crazy!"
Suzy giggled.

 *zzzZZZZIPP!*

Jack Quacker flew past them on his skateboard.

"Woo-hoo!" he shouted. "Second-grader coming through!"

"Look out!" Suzy called.

Jack whipped past a girl.

"Oh, no!" said Suzy. "That's my
new neighbor, Penelope O'Quinn.
Are you okay, Penelope?" she called.

"I'm all right," Penelope said.
Her voice was very soft.

Emily helped Penelope pick up
her lunch. *What an interesting lunch,*
thought Suzy. Olives. Tuna-and-
marshmallow sandwich. And a
green banana.

"Want to walk to school with us?" Suzy asked.

"That would be nice," said Penelope. *That would be great!* she thought. She didn't know many Duckport kids yet.

"I can't wait to meet our new teacher," Suzy said.

"I brought
her something,"
Penelope said
shyly. "See?"

"It sure is
...thorny,"
Emily noted.

"Thank you!" said Penelope.
"I wanted to get her something no
one else would."

At the schoolyard, the girls joined
a jump-rope game.

"Let's do the bubble-gum song,"
called Suzy.

Suddenly a voice boomed…

"BUBBLE GUM, BUBBLE GUM,
IN A DISH!
HOW MANY PIECES DO YOU WISH?
ONE! . . . TWO! . . . THREE! . . .
FOUR! . . . FIVE! . . . SIX! . . ."

Windows rattled.
Traffic stopped.
Penelope sure was full of surprises!

"I wonder if our new teacher will
be funny," said Jack.

"I wonder if she's strict," said
Corky Turtle.

"I wonder why she's not here yet,"
said Suzy.

BRRIIIIINNGG!

A bicycle bell rang behind them.

"Sorry I'm late!" the teacher sang out. "I stopped for donuts! Nothing kicks off the school year like a good cruller, I always say!"

"I am Ms. Cornelia O'Plume," she
announced. "But if you like, you may
call me Ms. O."

Ms. O pulled some very odd things out of her bag.

"Well, boys and girls," she began, "we have a very exciting year ahead of us."

"We are going to keep journals.
We are going to work with fractions.
And we are even going to build a city
out of snack crackers."

"Sometimes," Ms. O'Plume said, "we will stand on our heads. But mostly we are going to HAVE FUN."

"Now it's your turn. Suzy Ducken, would you please tell us about yourself?" Ms. O asked.

"Certainly, Ms. O'Plume," said Suzy. Folks always noticed Suzy's good manners. Ms. O did, too.

Suzy told about her
rock collection.

Then Jack showed his
latest skateboard move.

Corky said that he liked
maps. He liked Ms. O's
globe earrings.

Emily skipped her turn. She was
busy handing out napkins.
"Donuts can be so messy!" she said.

Finally it was Penelope's turn.

"My favorite color is brown because it goes with me," she began. "And my favorite snack is stuffed olives—because I like food that looks you in the eye."

"And I like being a porcupine
because I can put stuff on my quills!"
Her classmates laughed. They liked
this new kid.

"Time for art!" announced Ms. O.
"You'll be in three groups. I would like
you to create your very own leaf art."

"Think about expressing the beauty
of the season in a whole new way!
No idea is a bad idea."

"Let's think of something really cool," Suzy said to her friends.

"Let's wait and see what everybody else is doing," said Jack.

Emily scowled. "That's a bad idea."

"Ms. O said there are no bad ideas!" said Jack.

"Trust me!" said Suzy. "Copying is *always* a bad idea."

"I know what we could make," Penelope said softly.

She told everyone her plan.

All the groups were hard at work.
Finally Ms. O called out, "Finish up,
kids! It's show time!"

Vivian Snortwood's group went first.

"We put the leaves under the paper," said Vivian, "and then we rubbed crayons on the top."

"Very nice," Ms. O said. "I love the colors."

The next group unrolled their paper.
The trees on their picture were covered
with real leaves.

"I like the way you used those leaves,"
said Ms. O'Plume. "Next group!"

Suzy and her friends made a pile
of leaves in the middle of the floor.
All was quiet. Then Penelope called:
"I give you . . . FALL!"
Jack turned on the fan.

The leaves swirled all around.
It was like being outside on a windy
day! The children and Ms. O clapped
and clapped.

"Bravo!" said Ms. O. "Living art!
How wonderful!"

"Your idea was really different," Jack told Penelope, "but it turned out great!"

"Penelope's ideas *are* different," said Suzy. "And *that*'s what we like about her!"